Curtain Up!

A BOOK
FOR YOUNG PERFORMERS

BY DIRK McLEAN

Illustrated by

FRANCE BRASSARD

Tundra Books

For Renee, with love. - D.M.
To Roch and Dominique. - F.B.

Special thanks to Kathy and Lauren. Thanks to the Woodcock Fund and to
the memory of George & Ingeborg Woodcock.

Text copyright © 2010 by Dirk McLean
Illustrations copyright © 2010 by France Brassard

Published in Canada by Tundra Books,
75 Sherbourne Street, Toronto, Ontario M5A 2P9

Published in the United States by Tundra Books of Northern New York,
P.O. Box 1030, Plattsburgh, New York 12901

Library of Congress Control Number: 2009938452

Library and Archives Canada Cataloguing in Publication

McLean, Dirk, 1956-
            Curtain up! : A book for young performers / Dirk McLean ; illustrated by France Brassard.

For ages 6-8.
ISBN 978-0-88776-899-6

            1. Theater–Juvenile literature. 2. Theater–Production and direction–
Juvenile literature. I. Brassard, France, 1963- II. Title.

PN2037.M37 2010   j792   C2009-907389-7

We acknowledge the financial support of the Government of Canada through the Book Publishing Industry Development Program (BPIDP) and that
of the Government of Ontario through the Ontario Media Development Corporation's Ontario Book Initiative. We further acknowledge the support
of the Canada Council for the Arts and the Ontario Arts Council for our publishing program.

ONTARIO ARTS COUNCIL
CONSEIL DES ARTS DE L'ONTARIO

Printed and bound in China

1 2 3 4 5 6   15 14 13 12 11 10

Cast of Characters

ACTORS are the people who show and tell, using their voices and bodies,
the stories of others.

COSTUME DESIGNERS create the costumes that the actors wear, keeping in mind how
they are likely to move while on stage.

DIRECTORS interpret the script by ensuring all elements of the show come together in
the performance.

DRAMATURGES clarify and communicate the playwright's vision.

LIGHTING DESIGNERS decide on position, type, focus, direction, and color of the
lighting in every scene.

MUSIC COMPOSERS write all the music for the show, ensuring the songs match
the moods of each scene.

PLAYWRIGHTS conceive and write the story.

PRODUCERS are responsible for all of the business and administration of the production.
They raise the money and decide how it is spent.

PRODUCTION MANAGERS plan and coordinate the theatrical process and track the budget
for the show.

PROPERTY MASTERS make or acquire all the props for the play.

PUBLICISTS advertise the show, using information about the play and players.

SET DESIGNERS make sure the scenery and background of the show is accurate
and believable.

STAGE MANAGERS supervise everything and everyone in the backstage area. They
take control of the production after the dress rehearsal.

PROLOGUE

"Ten thousand teeny-tiny teacups teeter-totter on Tiffany's thumb," Amaya repeated. She knew she couldn't mumble during her monologue, so her mother had taught her the tongue twister to help her speak clearly.

Amaya loved to sing, she loved to dance, and she loved to act. This was the first time she had tried out for a big play – a musical. She wanted so much to be a part of this story about a girl celebrating her birthday in a park.

Hopeful girls crowded the hall, but when it was her turn to audition, Amaya stood alone in front of the director and stage manager. Her parents watched, off to the side.

"That was a beautiful monologue, Amaya. And so was your choice of song. I'd like you to come back and read for the lead role," said the director.

So she did. In fact, she auditioned a second *and* a third time. Amaya's excitement and nervousness made her feel dizzy. To keep the butterflies and knots away, she repeated her tongue twister, "Ten thousand teeny-tiny teacups teeter-totter on Tiffany's thumb."

The final audition was down to five kids. Amaya knew that only one of them would be chosen as the lead. *Which of us will it be?* she wondered.

ACT I

Waiting to hear seemed to take forever. She willed the phone to ring. When it finally did, the news was good. "I'm in the play!" Amaya said happily. She had been chosen to play the lead child. All of her singing and dancing and acting classes had paid off. Now, she and the other child actors would be in a professional play, rehearsing during the day and working with a tutor to keep up with their schoolwork.

On Amaya's first day of rehearsal, she arrived at the rehearsal hall and met the other actors and crew members. They played a game to learn each other's names and to get to know one another.

"Amaya – I love armadillos, asparagus pie, and apple juice!" she shouted, and she tossed the ball to the next person.

Then the actors read through the lines of the play together.

Halfway through the rehearsal, the director called out, "Break!" During the break, the set designer showed the cast and stage crew a miniature model of the set. To Amaya, the model looked as small as her favorite dollhouse.

Then the costume designer took the actors' measurements for their costumes. The costumes would help them feel like their characters.

A few days later, the director blocked all of the scenes. Amaya and the other actors waited as the stage manager taped off their new positions on the floor. This would help them to know where to stand onstage.

The choreographer showed the actors the dance moves. The actors repeated the steps until the choreographer was satisfied that they were learning them. Though she had danced before, Amaya had to learn new steps, and they were harder than they seemed. But slowly, with every new move, she began to feel more confident.

ACT II

At home, Amaya practiced her dialogue and gestures in front of her mother, her dolls, and her cat. Remembering the lines was hard. Her character was supposed to say "I used to have a yellow dress," but the words just wouldn't come. "*Mom*, I keep forgetting!"

"Saying your lines over and over is one way to remember them, Amaya. But you also need to picture what you're talking about." Her mother was a good coach. "Being able to understand what you're saying makes it easier for you to remember, and it will make your performance more believable to the audience."

"Okay, so I should picture the yellow dress while I say my line?"

"That's right!"

So that's what Amaya did.

That night, as Amaya slept, she dreamt that she was dancing on air, gliding across the set. Best of all, she didn't feel like Amaya. She felt like her character, and that felt wonderful.

The director had arranged for Amaya and the other young actors to go on a field trip to the shop, where the set was being built. The workers seemed intent on everything they were doing to build the fountain, the trees, and the benches that would make the audience feel they were in a park. Energy was in the air.

They visited the property master, who took them on a tour of the shop and introduced them to his team. Amaya felt like part of the team, too.

Amaya and the cast rehearsed in the rehearsal hall for
what seemed like forever but was only a couple of months.
Each time they practiced, the cast grew more comfortable
with each other and with their characters. It really began to show
in the performance.

Finally, the cast and stage crew moved into the theater and onto the real stage for the last few rehearsals. Together they toured the backstage area. The fountain, which they had first seen as a model, then as it was being constructed, was finished now, and it sat in the middle of the stage. The stage area was shaping up into a park.

There was only a week left until opening night, and Amaya and the other actors were onstage in front of their first audience. During this preview performance, Amaya went *dry*. She couldn't remember her line! Her mind went blank. She just couldn't picture a yellow dress. Amaya felt like running out of the theater.

Then somewhere in the background, she heard a whisper: "I used to have a yellow dress." The stage manager was *feeding* her the line! Amaya repeated it, feeling stronger as the show continued.

On opening night, Amaya said her favorite tongue twister and some new ones she had learned from the other actors. They helped her to control her stage fright. But she remembered forgetting her lines at the preview performance – there was an even bigger audience tonight!

Amaya knew her whole family was watching from the audience. The spotlights seemed to shine right through her. What if she forgot again!

But with every line, she felt herself loosening up. Amaya was at the park and not on a stage. She fell into her role, and the lines all seemed to come to her. As she looked around, everyone seemed to be having a great time. The performance went smoothly. Together, the cast took their curtain call.

After the show, Amaya and her guests attended the opening-night party with the cast and stage crew members. There were tables filled with food and drinks, and music blared in the background. There was a festive mood, with lots of hugs and laughter. Amaya could see how happy and proud her mother and father were for her. Everyone was thinking the same thing: *Would reviewers like it too?*

The next day, the play received terrific reviews. The cast did interviews for the local newspaper and TV station as cameras rolled and photographers clicked away.

EPILOGUE

maya knew her work wasn't over. She continued to practice at home and rehearse onstage before every performance to keep each show fresh and magical.

Swarmed by new fans, Amaya signed autographs. "Thank you for coming to our performance," she said.

Amaya looked forward to a long, long run of the play and to many more plays to come.

Glossary

AUDITION is where the actors try out for a part in a play, and it is like a job interview.

BACKSTAGE is the area behind the stage where actors enter and exit, and where workshops, storerooms, the green room, and dressing rooms are located.

BLOCKING is the way the director plans the physical movement of the play with the actors.

CHOREOGRAPHY is the movement and dance sequence in the show.

COSTUMES are the clothing that each character wears during the show.

GREEN ROOM is the actors' meeting space in the backstage area.

FRONT-OF-HOUSE is the front area of the theater house, which holds the box office and the lobby, where the audience can enjoy refreshments and purchase merchandise.

HOUSE is the auditorium, where the audience sits to watch the performance.

OPENING NIGHT is the first performance of the play.

PREVIEW PERFORMANCES have all of the technical parts of a regular show. Tickets are sold at a discount price so the cast and crew can test out the play in front of an audience.

PROPS are small articles used by actors onstage.

REVIEWS are written by critics who work for newspapers, magazines, television stations, and other media outlets.

SETS are the physical background seen by the audience, which show where the story takes place. They can be fixed in place or wheeled on and off stage.

STAGE DOOR is a separate entrance and exit used only by the cast and crew.